The Littlest Christmas Elf

By Nancy Buss
Illustrated by Terri Super

Western Publishing Company, Inc. offers a wide variety of children's videos, tapes and games.

For information write to:
Western Publishing Company, Inc.
1220 Mound Avenue
Racine, WI 53404

D1532778

A GOLDEN BOOK • NEW YORK
Western Publishing Company, Inc., Racine, Wisconsin 53404

Allister the elf was excited. Today he was leaving for the North Pole. The whole village of Elfin Corners had come to say good-bye. Even the mayor was there.

"This year Santa has sent for our merriest elf to join his workshop," the mayor said. "We will miss Allister's songs and stories. Yet Santa needs the best, and our Allister is a very special elf!"

But when Allister arrived at the North Pole, he didn't feel special at all. He was the littlest elf there. He was so tiny that the head elf, McCafferty, couldn't find him a job.

McCafferty gave Allister a wagon to build, but Allister was too small to hammer.

He gave him a dollhouse to paint, but Allister couldn't reach the roof.

He gave him some bears to stuff, but that didn't work either. "He's buried beneath them!" said the elf in charge of bears.

McCafferty shook his head. "Just two weeks until
Christmas, and we still have so much work to do. We have
to find you a job. Perhaps you can sweep."

But even the broom was too big for Allister, and the
other elves began to laugh.

"Why, he's just a runt!" said one elf. He poked a friend and giggled.

"He's smaller than I am," said another, who stuck out his tongue.

"And absolutely useless," said a third. "Santa should send him away."

Allister blinked his eyes quickly so he wouldn't cry. "I don't belong here," he thought. "I'm so little even Santa won't like me."

Then he pushed through the crowd and ran from the room. "But Santa *won't* send me away," said Allister, "because he will never see me."

Allister kept running until he found a perfect place to
hide—down behind the woodpile, in back of the reindeer
pen. It was there that Allister found a friend.

"My name is Nicholas," said an old elf, peering over the
woodpile. "What's yours?"

Allister answered in a whisper.

Nicholas shook his hand. "I'm glad to know you," he
said. "Would you like to help me with the reindeer?"

When Allister nodded, Nicholas lifted him up to his shoulders, and the two of them chattered and sang while they fed and watered the reindeer.

Allister was so happy to find a friend that he returned
to the reindeer pen the next day and the next. Nicholas
never minded if Allister asked questions, and he never
told Allister he was too small to help.

While Nicholas cleaned out the stalls Allister fed the
reindeer apples. While Nicholas brushed a reindeer's coat
Allister polished harness bells. And all the while he told
Nicholas stories, and together they sang to the reindeer.

But one morning Nicholas was gone. Someone else was hauling the water. Someone else was cleaning the pen.

"Where is Nicholas?" Allister asked.

"Nicholas, indeed!" said a grumpy elf who was busily swinging a pitchfork. "He's up at the big house. Now go away. I have work to do."

"The big house!" thought Allister. "But that's where Santa lives! Nicholas must be sick. He must be very sick if he's staying with Santa." And the thought of his friend in that big scary house sent Allister scurrying home to the safety of his bed.

But he didn't sleep. He was worried about Nicholas. And he missed him so much, he knew he'd have to see him.

So the next morning, Allister packed a basket of fruit and started out for a visit. But the nearer he got to Santa's house, the slower his steps became. Finally he stopped completely, behind a Christmas tree in Santa's front yard. His heart was beating loudly.

Suddenly the door opened, and Allister, more frightened than ever, dived beneath the pine tree. He heard footsteps, and he buried his head under his arms. The footsteps came closer. Allister was afraid to breathe. He closed his eyes tightly and prayed that no one would see him.

But someone jiggled his foot. "Hey, there," said a voice, "you're not hurt, are you?"

Allister let out a long, slow breath. He peeked out from under his arms. IT WAS NICHOLAS! Allister scurried out from under the tree and gave his friend a hug.

"Well, it's Allister. I've missed you! And how are my reindeer? The week before Christmas is so busy, I don't have time to take care of them. Come inside and talk to me."

And before Allister could say a word, his friend had
hoisted him to his shoulders and begun walking toward
the house.

"No, no!" Allister cried. "I can't go in there. Put me
down!" And he wiggled and squirmed so much that the
old elf did.

"Can't go in where?" Nicholas asked.
Allister pointed toward the house.
"And why not, may I ask?"
"Because Santa won't like me, and he'll send me home."

"Why would he do that?" asked Nicholas.

"Because I'm little, and I can't do anything right, and—"

The old elf interrupted. "Why, that's nonsense," he said. "You're a big help to me. In fact, I have a special job just for you."

"A special job?" asked Allister. "For me?"

"Exactly right," said Nicholas. "You're coming with me this year when I make my deliveries."

"Deliveries?" said Allister.

"The toys—the toys to the children on Christmas Eve," said Nicholas. "You see, it's a long trip, and I get lonely. But you could come with me, Allister. You're so small, you'll fit in the sleigh. And you could tell me stories, and we could sing songs, just like we do in the reindeer pen."

Allister's mouth dropped open. His eyes got big and round. "Then you're Santa Claus."

His friend bowed. "Also known as Saint Nicholas."

Allister began to back away. Then he stopped and grinned. "But I'm not afraid of you."

"I'm glad," said the old elf. "Will you come with me on Christmas Eve?"

"Oh, yes," said Allister.

That's exactly what he did. And it was the best
Christmas Eve Allister — or Santa — ever had.